ENDANGERED Fairytails

Goldiscales
and the Three Honey Badgers

A Retelling of the Classic Fairytale
Goldilocks and the Three Bears

featuring the endangered species:
Manis tricuspis (Pangolin)

Lee Wilder

illustrated by
Jeffrey Moss

kris & co.

PRESS

Paperback
ISBN 978-1-7359103-7-6

Kris & Co. Press
P.O. Box 5102
Mesa, Arizona 85211

Printed in the USA   First Printing 2021

"And then she went to the porridge of the Little Wee Bear, and tasted it, and that was neither too hot nor too cold, but just right."

Goldilocks and the Three Bears
Flora Annie Steel

Dedicated to Eleanor

Momma Honey Badger had just finished making three delicious bowls of ants and honey.

"I'm not hungry!" Baby Honey Badger wailed.

"Why don't we go for a walk?
I'm sure that will give you an appetite,"
said Papa Honey Badger.

The three honey badgers left for their evening walk, not prepared for the mischief coming their way.

Goldiscales, a young pangolin,
had snuck away from her mother's
back to explore the savannah.

She was having fun
wandering through the underbrush,
looking at every insect and tree
and rock.

Soon, Goldiscales' stomach
began to rumble.

"I need to find something
to eat," she said to herself.

When she came across a hole,
she called,

"Hello?"

Then, as she leaned over to peek into the hole,
she lost her balance.

Tumbling and rolling, she went down the tunnel of dirt, finally landing in a little room with a table and three chairs.

She crept closer to investigate and found three bowls on the table, each full of honey and ants. What a treat!

Goldiscales stuck out her long, sticky tongue and tried the first bowl.

"Too sweet!" she said, wrinkling her nose.

She shuffled along and tried the next one.

"Too salty!" she said, pushing the bowl away.

She moved on to the very last one.

"This one is juuust right!" Goldiscales liked it so much, she ate the whole thing.

With a belly full of
tasty food, she wandered
into another room in
the tunnel, this one
full of sticks.

Goldiscales
loved sticks!

With her long, sharp fingernails, they were fun to pull apart, and sometimes they had treats inside. She tried the first stick.

"This one is too big."

She grabbed the second stick and nibbled on the end.

"This one is too small."

She got to the last stick.

"This one is juuust right! It even has some termites in it. Yum!"

Goldiscales took the third stick apart, making sure she got each and every bug.

Next, Goldiscales went to see if there was somewhere she could take a nap before heading home.

She found one last room lined with cozy fur – the perfect place for a nap! Inside the room were three little dips in the earth, perfect for a little pangolin to curl up in.

Goldiscales tried the first one.

"This one is much too deep," she said, as she rolled around.

Goldiscales tried the second one .

"This one is too shallow."

But the last one was a perfect fit.

"This one is warm and cozy. It's juuust right!"

Goldiscales rolled into a ball and snuggled in to go to sleep. Just a quick nap, and then she would go back to find her mother.

Around that time, the three honey badgers came home from their walk, hungry for dinner. But, when they sat down to eat, they noticed something was wrong.

"Hey!" said Papa Honey Badger.
"Someone has been eating my food."

"Someone ate some of my food too!"
said Momma Honey Badger.

"Someone ate my food too!
It's all gone!"

wailed Baby Honey Badger.

The three shared what was left, but their
stomachs still growled with hunger.

When they went to relax in their chewing stick room,
they discovered something else was wrong.

"Someone touched my chewing stick,"

said Papa Honey Badger.

"Someone touched my chewing stick too,"

said Momma Honey Badger.

"Someone touched my chewing stick too, and now it's broken!"

Baby Honey Badger began to sob.

Momma Honey Badger held him
until he calmed down.

"There, there. How about we go to bed?
I'm sure you will feel better in the morning."

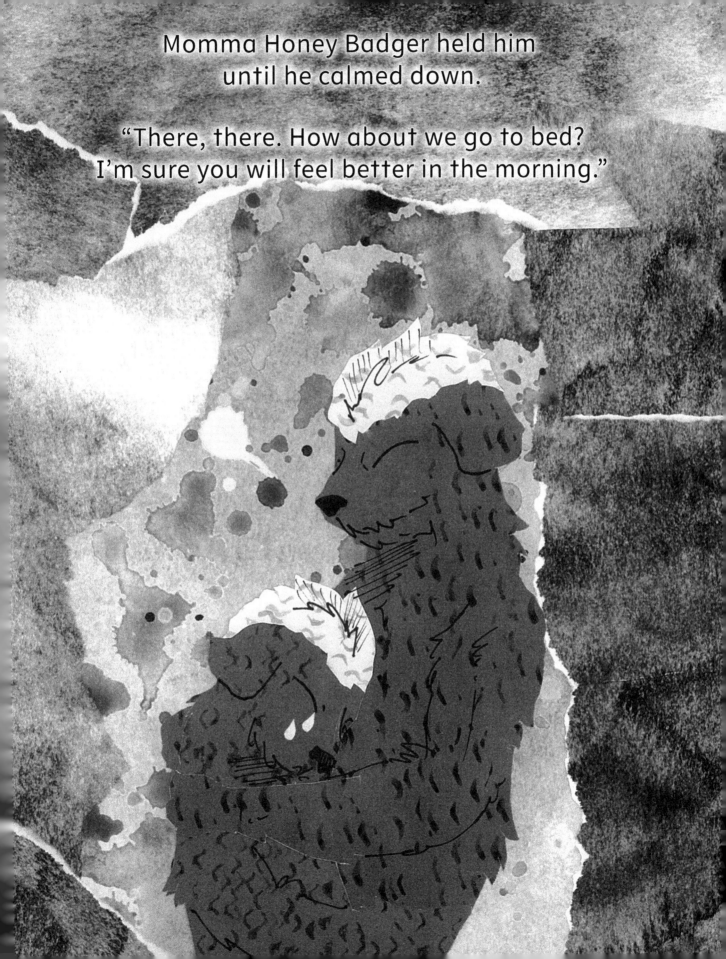

The three honey badgers all agreed and went into their sleeping den.

"Someone has been sleeping in my bed!" said Papa Honey Badger.

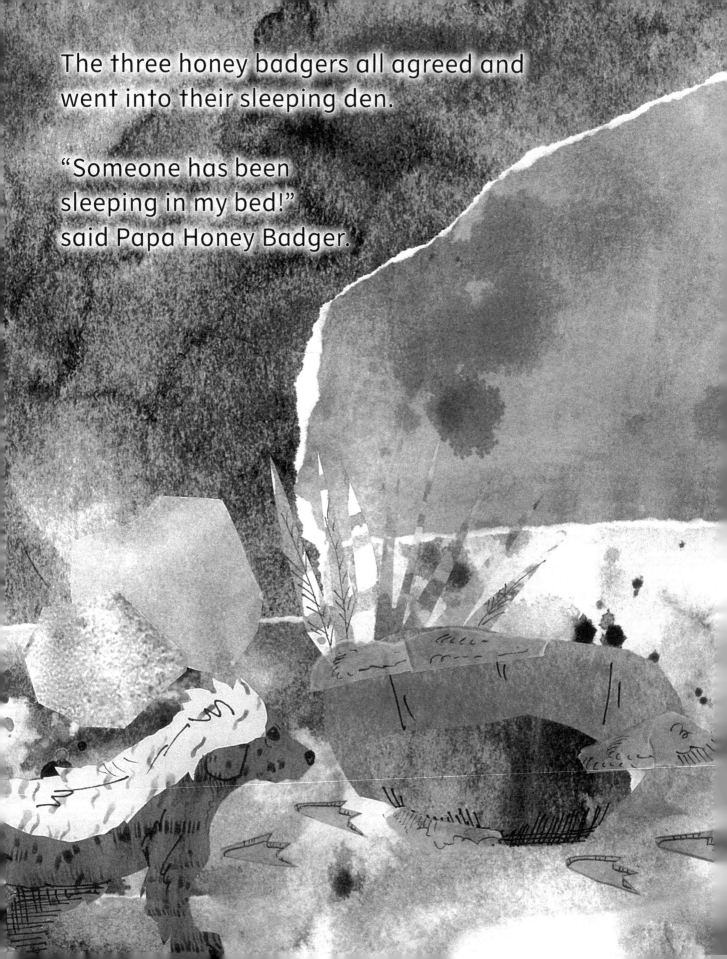

"Someone has been sleeping in my bed too!" said Momma Honey Badger.

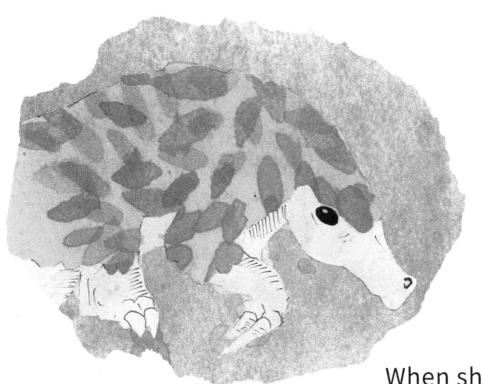

When she saw
the three honey badgers,
she ran out of the sleeping den,

past the
chewing sticks,

past the table with the empty bowls,

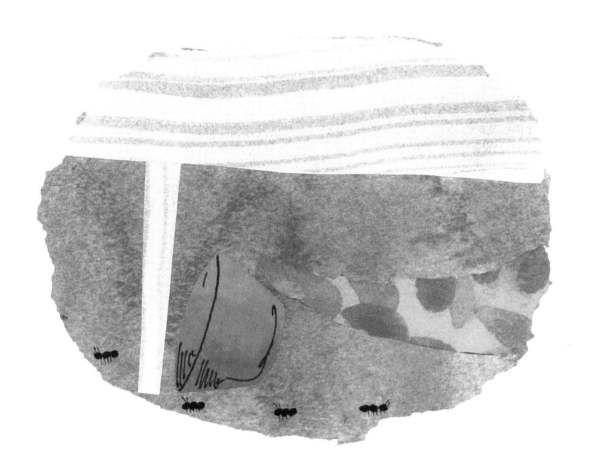

and up the tunnel back into the savannah.

Goldiscales ran and ran.

In fact, she ran right into her mother, who had been frantically looking for her.

"Goldiscales, I have been so worried! Where have you been?" her mother asked.

Goldiscales climbed up to her spot on her mother's tail and hugged it tight.

"Oh Momma, you would not believe the day I have had."

Her mother started walking home as Goldiscales told her mother all about her adventure.

Pangolin Facts

Pangolins can curl up in a tight ball, like an armadillo.

Pangolin scales are made of the same stuff as human fingernails and hair, but are strong enough to protect them from predators.

Pangolins like to eat bugs such as ants and termites.

When they are eating, pangolins can close their ears and nose to keep bugs out.

Pangolins are very shy and like lots of alone time.

Baby pangolins will spend most of their time riding around on their mother's tail.

Pangolins are found in the forests and savannahs of Asia and Africa.

Did you know?

Honey Badgers got their name because of their sweet tooth. They will eat almost anything, but their favorite thing is honey.

Honey Badgers are very protective of their homes. If you ever see one in the wild, you should walk away.

Deer
Honee
Badgers,

Im Sorry

Bibliography

Absolon, J., Cundall, J., & Weir, H. (1850). The Story of the Three Bears. In The Treasury of pleasure books for young children (pp. 217-232). London, England: Grant and Griffith and Joseph Cundall. doi:https://en.wikisource.org/wiki/A_Treasury_of_Pleasure_Books_for_Young_Children/The_Story_of_the_Three_Bears

Honey badger. (2020, September 9). Retrieved September 28, 2020, from https://en.wikipedia.org/wiki/Honey_badger

Panesar, B. (2020, August 22). Honey badgers: Adorable but fierce little mammals. Retrieved September 28, 2020, from https://www.livescience.com/honey-badger.html

Pangolins. (2019, April 10). Retrieved September 28, 2020, from https://www.nationalgeographic.com/animals/mammals/group/pangolins/ Pangolins. (2019, December 18). Retrieved September 28, 2020, from https://www.pangolinsg.org/pangolins/

Steel, F. A. (1918). Goldilocks and the Three Bears. In English Fairy Tales. essay.

What is a pangolin? (2020). Retrieved September 28, 2020, from https://www.worldwildlife.org/stories/what-is-a-pangolin

ABOUT THE AUTHOR

LEE WILDER is a redhead and therefore technically an endangered species herself. She is a desert-based author living her dream with her pack of rescue animals, including four cats and a dog. As a hobby, she enjoys book binding, sharing her love of animals, and baking for her friends.

ABOUT THE SERIES

ENDANGERED FAIRYTAILS strives to inspire a love of classic children's stories in young readers as well as raise awareness about endangered animals. Together, we can make the world a better place!

More by Lee Wilder

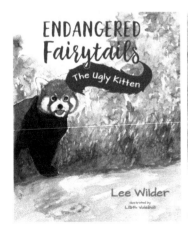

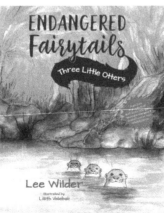

TO FIND OUT MORE

VISIT
leewilderbooks.com

FOLLOW
@endangered_fairytails
on Instagram

CPSIA information can be obtained
at www.ICGtesting.com
Printed in the USA
BVHW052216091121
621202BV00016B/299

9 781735 910376